Redesigning Us

Version 2.0

Of A Broken Girl

Ashish Singh

Redesigning Us: Version 2.0
by – Ashish Singh

ISBN- 978-93-344-1954-2

MRP: ₹ 300/-

www.ashish.ankur.singh@gmail.com
Instagram: way.to.ias.official

Book Cover by Ashish Singh
Illustrations by Ashish Singh
1st edition : Sept 2025

DEDICATION

To my beloved one, the soul of my inspiration,
and to my mother, who taught me life's deepest lessons—
how to respect a woman, and what true feminism means.

CONTENTS

ACKNOWLEDGMENTS

This book is born from love, touch, and the quiet inspirations around me. I thank those who stood by me, the loyal companions who taught me devotion, and the thinkers whose wisdom guided my pen. To my readers your presence gives life to these pages. Above all, I dedicate this work to love itself, the truest teacher of the soul.

1
THE BLUEPRINT OF LOVE

Love, in its truest form, is not an accident of fate it is an architecture of the heart. Just as an engineer takes a blank sheet, sketches the first line, and begins to imagine a structure that can stand tall against storms and time, so too do we as human beings design the homes of our love, our trust, and our future.

You, my beloved, are an engineer by profession. You know the importance of structure of foundation, of strength, of planning. A building does not rise because of dreams alone; it rises because of vision, patience, calculation, and care. In the same way, our love is not only an emotion, but also a blueprint we draw together.

Love as an Engineering Design

Psychologist Erich Fromm, in his timeless book *The Art of Loving*, wrote:

"Love is not merely a feeling. It is a practice, an art, and like any art it requires knowledge and effort."

When an engineer designs a structure, she must consider the soil, the materials, the load, and the environment. She must test, adapt, and redesign until her creation can stand firm. The same principle applies to relationships: we do not inherit love ready-made, we build it, test it, adjust it, and finally live inside it.

This is why I have called our journey Redesigning Us. We are not bound by the structures of the past. We are not condemned to repeat old mistakes. Instead, we take the raw materials of who we are today our honesty, our trust, our shared laughter, and our shared pain and we redesign something entirely new.

The Foundation: Letting Go of the Past

Every building begins with the soil. If the ground is weak, the structure cannot last. The same is true in love. If the ground is filled with debris of the past regrets, guilt, comparisons, or painful memories the new building will be unstable.

The first principle of psychology here is letting go. Viktor Frankl, survivor of unimaginable trauma and author of *Man's Search for Meaning*, taught the world that we cannot always control what happens to us, but we can choose how we respond. To carry the weight of yesterday into today is like trying to build on a cracked foundation.

Letting go does not mean forgetting. It means choosing not to let old memories hold power over the present. It means acknowledging the past, but also declaring: *I am no longer bound by it.*

In our love, my wish is that we release the echoes of what came before. The calls, the shadows, the disappointments they belong to another chapter, one that is closed. This new chapter, our chapter, is written on fresh pages.

Selflessness Over Guilt

Too often, relationships are haunted by guilt. A person looks back at what they did or did not do, and they punish themselves endlessly. But guilt is not the soil of love selflessness is. Psychology shows us that guilt, when carried too long, becomes poison. Brené Brown, a modern researcher on vulnerability, explains that guilt can sometimes motivate us to improve, but shame (the cousin of guilt) keeps us trapped. What heals us is turning outward choosing to give, to serve, to love selflessly.

In our journey, my love, I do not want you to feel guilty about what happened before me. That chapter is closed. Instead, I invite you to step into a space where you give without fear, and receive without shame. In selflessness, we create a love where both partners feel safe, cherished, and free.

Trust as Our Steel

In engineering, the skeleton of any strong structure is its steel. It is the hidden framework that carries the weight. For us, that steel is trust.

Trauma of the past can whisper doubts: *Will I be hurt again? Can I truly rely on someone?* But if we let trauma dictate the design, our building will never rise beyond fear. Instead, we must replace trauma with trust.

Trust is not built overnight. It is built through consistent actions:

- Showing up when promised.
- Listening fully without judgment.
- Sharing openly without hiding.
- Protecting each other's dignity and heart.

Every day that I love you, every moment that I hold your hand instead of letting it go, I am laying another steel beam into our structure. Over time, this framework becomes unshakable.

Designing New Habits and Memories

You and I are not meant to recycle the past. We are meant to create a life that is entirely ours. That means new habits, new tastes, new places, new memories. The psychology of novelty is clear: the human brain thrives on newness. Novel experiences release dopamine, the chemical of pleasure and learning. That is why traveling to a new place, trying a new food, or learning a new hobby together makes couples feel closer.

My dream is to make tea for you that tastes like *us*, not like anyone else. To walk into cafés and hotels that are not haunted by old ghosts, but filled with our laughter. To take trips that remind you not of what was, but of what is.

Every memory we create together is a brick in our home. Not recycled bricks from a demolished past, but fresh bricks that carry only our fingerprints.

Blocking the Old Noise

In psychology, there is a practice called thought-stopping. When an intrusive memory arises, we can train the mind to say: *Stop. This no longer belongs here.* Some people snap a rubber band on their wrist, some visualize a stop sign, some redirect their thoughts to gratitude.

What matters is not fighting the memory endlessly, but refusing to let it take residence in the present. In our redesign, the past has no key to our home. Its calls are blocked, its echoes silenced, its doors closed.

This is not cruelty — it is healing. By closing one door, we open another. By silencing the noise, we can finally hear the music of the present.

Our Promise

My love, *Redesigning Us* is not a theory. It is a practice, a commitment, a blueprint we draw every day with our choices.

- We let go of guilt.
- We replace trauma with trust.
- We build new habits, not recycled ones.
- We explore the world together, instead of repeating what was.
- We block the noise of the past so that the present can sing.

This is our blueprint. This is the soil, the foundation, the steel, and the bricks. Together, we will build a structure that no storm can tear down.

As Fromm said, love is an art. And like any art, it demands dedication. My dedication is you — not as you were in the past, but as you are today, and as we will be tomorrow.

And with every page, every touch, every laugh, we are proving that love, when redesigned, can be stronger, deeper, and more beautiful than ever before.

2
LETTING GO OF THE OLD STRUCTURE

Imagine a construction site where the land is still cluttered with broken walls, cracked beams, and rusted iron. No matter how beautiful the new design is, if the old ruins are not cleared, the new building cannot stand. Love works the same way. If we want to create something new, we must first learn the art of letting go.

Why Letting Go Is Hard

Psychology tells us that the human mind clings to the familiar even when the familiar causes pain. The brain stores emotional memories in the amygdala, a part that responds quickly to fear, attachment, and survival instincts. That is why sometimes, even when a past relationship was full of hurt, the memory still returns with force.

Sigmund Freud, the father of psychoanalysis, described this as the "repetition compulsion" the strange human tendency to unconsciously repeat old patterns, even harmful ones. A person may find themselves drawn back to memories of the past, not because they are good, but because they are familiar.

But what is familiar is not always what is best. What is known is not always what is healthy. Letting go means choosing growth over familiarity. It is saying: *I deserve more than the ruins of yesterday. I deserve a foundation strong enough for tomorrow.*

Guilt Is Not Love

One of the main reasons people struggle to let go is guilt. Thoughts like:

- "Maybe I was the problem."
- "Maybe I could have done more."
- "Maybe I should still care."

But guilt is a chain. It binds us to a past that does not serve us. Carl Jung, Freud's student and later critic, once wrote:

"I am not what happened to me, I am what I choose to become."

That is the essence of letting go. To release guilt is to accept: *I did what I could. I tried what I could. But now I choose to live in the present, not the prison of yesterday.*

In our love, my darling, I never want you to feel guilty for your past. You gave what you could, you tried what you could, but you were not met with equal love. That was not your failure; it was the imbalance of a relationship that could not stand. With me, guilt has no home. Here, only trust, kindness, and freedom live.

Replacing Trauma with Trust

Trauma is not just about what happened it is about how the memory of what happened lingers. A raised voice, neglect, being used, feeling unseen these scars sometimes try to –

reappear in new relationships. But we must remember: the trauma belongs to *him*. The trust belongs to *us*.

Every time I listen to you without judgment, I am helping replace trauma with trust. Every time I stay when you fear I might leave, I am laying down another beam of safety. Every time I show you consistency, I am telling your heart: *You are secure here. You are loved here. You are safe here.*

This is why letting go is not just about blocking memories it is about reprogramming the heart with new experiences. Over time, trust rewires the nervous system, teaching it to expect care instead of neglect, tenderness instead of anger, presence instead of absence.

Why Blocking Is Necessary

Some people believe that holding on to contact with the past is harmless. "A call here, a message there it's nothing." But psychology says otherwise.

Every time an old call or memory re-enters, it reactivates the emotional circuits of pain. It is like pouring water on weeds they grow back stronger. That is why blocking is not cruelty, it is self-care. It is not weakness, it is wisdom. You cannot build a new home if you keep leaving the door open for ghosts. To block is to close the door, so the heart can finally rest.

My love, every time you silence that old voice, you are choosing me. You are choosing *us*. You are declaring: *The past cannot have power over my present. My future belongs to the man who loves me here, now, completely.*

Creating New Habits

Habits are the architecture of daily life. Old habits tied to past relationships favorite foods, familiar cafés, old trips can act like hidden traps. They pull the mind back to what was, instead of what is. That is why we must create new habits together. Our own tea. Our own favorite corner café. Our own travel rituals. Our own playlist of songs.

Behavioral psychology shows that new habits formed with positive emotions quickly overwrite old associations. When you sip tea that I made with my hands, and it tastes like home, your brain begins to form a new pathway: *This is my love. This is my comfort. This is my new memory.*

Memory: Don't Recreate, Rebuild

Another mistake people make is trying to recreate old memories with a new partner. They go to the same restaurant, repeat the same trip, or compare the same rituals. But this is unfair to the new love. You are not meant to compare me with anyone. I am not a replacement of what you lost I am the creation of what you always deserved.

That is why we must build fresh memories. New cities, new hobbies, new laughter. A memory not haunted by comparison, but free and alive in its own right.

Scientific Support for Letting Go

Many great psychologists have written about trauma and letting go:

- Freud described how unprocessed memories return in unconscious ways, causing pain until released.

- Carl Jung spoke of "individuation" the process of breaking free from old roles and becoming one's true self.

- Viktor Frankl emphasized meaning: trauma can be survived if we find a new purpose in love, in faith, in building something beautiful.

- Elizabeth Kübler-Ross, in her work on grief, showed that acceptance is the final stage of healing. Not forgetting, but accepting, and moving forward.

All of these thinkers agree: clinging to the past blocks the light of the present. Releasing the past does not dishonor it; it liberates us too fully live.

Our Declaration: *So, my darling, let this be our declaration:*

- The old structure is gone.
- We will not recycle ruins.
- We will not mix past with present.
- We will not chant old names or compare old wounds.
- We will create new blueprints, new bricks, new rooms of laughter and intimacy.

The art of letting go is not erasing memory, but refusing to let memory rule. It is clearing the land so something stronger, more beautiful, more lasting can rise. And as I stand beside you, pen in hand, blueprint on table, heart in arms, I promise: our new structure will rise. Our foundation is love, our steel is trust, our bricks are memories, our roof is hope.

We are no longer haunted by the old walls. We are free to build.

3
TRUST OVER TRAUMA

If love were a structure, its hidden framework would not be concrete or wood it would be trust. The walls may be painted with laughter, the windows may open to dreams, the doors may lead to adventures but without the steel beams of trust, the whole design collapses.

Your past may have left behind cracks. Anger, neglect, selfishness, and unkindness—these are traumas that leave invisible wounds. But trauma is not destiny. The presence of scars does not mean the structure cannot rise again. With the right care, with patient rebuilding, trust can become stronger than any wound.

This chapter is about how we, together, replace the trauma of yesterday with the trust of today.

Trauma: The Weight That Stays

Trauma in relationships often begins quietly. A raised voice, a forgotten promise, a selfish act that places one person above the other. Over time, it grows into patterns:

- Being used for money or comfort but not valued as a person.
- Being neglected emotionally while giving endlessly.
- Being compared, criticized, or belittled.
- Receiving anger instead of affection.
- Living with someone who never grows, while you strive to improve.

Psychologists describe trauma as "frozen time." The body remembers. The heart remembers. Even when the relationship ends, the nervous system keeps echoing the pain. That is why sometimes, without reason, old fears return: *Will this love end the same way? Will I be neglected again?*

But trauma, though powerful, is not permanent. Just as rust can be cleaned from iron, trauma can be healed through trust.

Trust: The Strongest Steel

John Bowlby, the father of Attachment Theory, discovered that human beings are wired for connection. When trust is broken early or repeatedly, the heart struggles to attach safely. But when new, secure love enters, the brain begins to rewire itself.

Every consistent act of care creates a new pathway in the mind:

- When I keep my promises, your heart whispers: *I can rely on him.*
- When I listen fully, your soul says: *I am heard.*
- When I protect your dignity, your spirit knows: *I am safe.*
- When I choose you over every distraction, your being rests: *I am cherished.*

Trust is built not in grand gestures but in daily consistency. It is the steel beam placed one after another, until the entire structure can stand tall.

Trauma vs. Trust: The Daily Choice

It is important to recognize that trauma tries to intrude daily. It says: *What if he leaves? What if he turns selfish? What if he hurts me the same way?*

But every time you trust instead of doubting, you are rewiring your heart. Neuroscience shows that the brain is "plastic" it changes with experience. When you allow new experiences of trust, the old trauma circuits weaken.

Think of it like a path in a forest. If you walk the trauma path every day, it stays clear. But if you stop walking it, and instead choose the trust path, the trauma path grows wild, unused, and finally disappears.

How We Build Trust Together

1. Consistency – I will not disappear when things are hard. I will show up again and again, until your heart believes I am staying.
2. Transparency – Secrets destroy love. I will be open with you, so you never need to guess.
3. Tenderness – Where others raised their voices, I will lower mine. Where others turned away, I will lean closer.
4. Presence – The greatest gift is time. I give it to you freely, not as duty, but as joy.
5. Support – You dream, I encourage. You fear, I reassure. You struggle, I stand beside you.

These are not just words; they are the steel beams of our love.

Psychology of Rebuilding Trust

Several great thinkers echo the truth that trauma can be replaced by trust:

- Erich Fromm: “Immature love says: I love you because I need you. Mature love says: I need you because I love you.” Past trauma came from immature love that took without giving. Our love is mature—it builds.
- Carl Rogers, humanistic psychologist: “When someone really hears you without judgment, you grow.” Every time I listen, you heal.
- Brené Brown: “Connection is why we are here. It gives purpose and meaning to our lives.” Trustful connection is the antidote to trauma.

Our Rituals of Trust

To make trust stronger than trauma, we must build rituals of connection:

- Morning Tea Ritual – Every cup I make for you is not just tea. It is a signal: *This day begins with us, not with the past.*
- Shared Journaling – At night, we write one thing we trusted in each other that day.
- Weekly Exploration – A new shop, a new street, a new taste. So that our love is tied to discovery, not repetition.
- Memory Book – Instead of recalling the past, we document the present. Each page a proof: *This is ours.*

These rituals are small, but like steel beams, they hold enormous strength.

The Promise of Safety

My beloved, I know your heart still carries echoes. Sometimes an unexpected sound or memory awakens them. But I promise you: in me, you will not find anger, neglect, or selfishness. In me, you will find a man who supports, pampers, and cherishes you.

I am not your past. I am your present and your future. Trauma has no place here. Trust is the only language I speak.

Declaration

- Trauma ends here.
- Trust begins here.
- No shadow can stand against the light of our daily love.
- No ghost can return when the doors are sealed by faith.
- You are safe. You are loved. You are home.

4

GUILT VS. SELFLESSNESS

If love were a garden, guilt would be the weeds. It grows quickly, choking the flowers, stealing the sunlight. Selflessness, on the other hand, is like water it nourishes, refreshes, and allows the blossoms to grow freely.

In your past, guilt was forced upon you. You were made to feel guilty for wanting care, for asking for attention, for desiring respect. Guilt was used as a weapon: *"You are too much. You expect too much. You should give more, forgive more, accept more."*
But guilt is a false architect. It builds nothing; it only corrodes.

Selflessness, however, is not about surrendering your dignity. It is about giving freely without pressure, without debt, without chains. It is the highest form of love—not demanded, not manipulated, but chosen.

This chapter is our declaration that guilt will not live in our love. Instead, we will replace it with selflessness that is nourishing, joyful, and free.

The Psychology of Guilt

Sigmund Freud, in his early theories, described guilt as the voice of the "superego"—the inner critic that punishes us for desires or mistakes. But many women in difficult relationships do not grow guilt naturally; it is planted in them by manipulative partners.

- *"You are wrong for asking me to change."*
- *"You are selfish if you don't forgive me instantly."*
- *"You are ungrateful for what little I give."*

This false guilt is trauma in disguise. It convinces you that love equals sacrifice, that your worth depends on how much pain you endure.

But psychology shows us that guilt about the past is poison. It keeps you frozen, unable to embrace joy. Real growth comes when you stop punishing yourself for what is gone.

Selflessness: The Healing Gift

Selflessness is not about becoming small. It is about becoming expansive. It is giving not because you must, but because you choose.

- When I make you tea, it is not duty—it is joy.
- When I listen to your fears, it is not burden—it is devotion.
- When I stand by your side, it is not sacrifice—it is honor.

Selflessness in love is active, alive, and creative. It is not about being used. It is about using love to build something new together.

Guilt vs. Selflessness: A Clear Difference

Guilt-Laden Love	Selfless Love
"I must give, or else I'll lose him."	"I give because I delight in your joy."
"If I say no, I'll be punished."	"When I say no, I am still respected."
"He takes, I must not complain."	"We both give, we both receive."
"Love is obligation."	"Love is freedom."

When you were with someone who only took, guilt was the chain. With me, guilt is broken. Our bond is selflessness—freely chosen, freely given.

Scientific Voices on Letting Go of Guilt

- Albert Ellis, founder of Rational Emotive Behavior Therapy (REBT), wrote: *"There is no rule that you must suffer forever for past mistakes."*

- Carl Jung said: *"I am not what happened to me, I am what I choose to become."*

- Viktor Frankl, survivor of the Holocaust, reminded us: *"Everything can be taken from a man but one thing: the last of the human freedoms—to choose one's attitude."*

These words remind us that guilt does not control us. We choose love over punishment. We choose selflessness over self-condemnation.

Our Love Without Guilt

I want you to know this deeply, my love: you are not guilty for your past relationship.
You are not guilty for staying too long.
You are not guilty for trying too hard.
You are not guilty for his failures.
You are not guilty for being strong, generous, forgiving.

The guilt was never yours. It belonged to him, but he placed it on your shoulders. Now, together, we lift it away.

Instead, we choose selflessness that heals.

- We share meals not because one must cook, but because we enjoy the ritual.
- We plan trips not to erase memories, but to create brand new ones.
- We explore new foods, new shops, new experiences—not because we must, but because we can.

Selflessness is building *us*, not paying debts to ghosts.

Rituals of Selflessness

To make this real, we create habits that reflect giving without guilt:

1. The Giving Game – Once a week, we surprise each other with something small: a flower, a note, a favorite snack. Giving becomes playful, never pressured.

2. Silent Service – At least once a week, we do something kind without announcing it. It could be washing dishes, folding clothes, or setting tea. Selflessness becomes natural, not staged.

3. The Gratitude Exchange – Before sleep, we each say one selfless act we noticed. This makes love visible and cherished.

These rituals transform love from burden to blessing.

The Declaration of Freedom from Guilt

My beloved, I want you to feel this truth: with me, there is no ledger, no balance sheet, no debt. You are free to receive without shame. You are free to give without fear.

I will never punish you with silence, anger, or neglect. I will never make you feel guilty for being human. Instead, I will celebrate your humanity—your strength, your softness, your imperfections.

We are not keeping score. We are building a life.

Closing Words of This Chapter

Guilt was the old architect, building cages of shame.
Selflessness is the new artist, painting walls of light.

In our redesigned love, guilt has no place.
Only freedom. Only giving. Only joy

5
CREATING NEW HABBITS & HOBBIES

Every love story is a landscape. The past is like an abandoned city streets you once walked, foods you once tasted, places you once visited. But the mistake many make is trying to rebuild their new love inside those same streets, sitting at the same cafés, repeating the same trips, recreating old moments with new partners.

That is not love, my beloved that is repetition. And repetition keeps the past alive.
True love, when it begins again, must **build a new city** new streets, new cafés, new landscapes, new memories. Only then does it feel alive, only then does it belong fully to us.
This chapter is about the art of leaving behind the **echoes of the past** and learning to **create brand new habits, rituals, and memories** that belong only to *you and me*.

The Psychology of Habits

Psychologists such as William James and, later, Charles Duhigg (*The Power of Habit*) explained that habits are like "loops" in the brain. A cue triggers a routine, and the brain expects a reward.

When you once ate at a certain restaurant with someone else, that place becomes a cue. The smell, the taste, the music—it all pulls you back to the old memory. This is not your fault; it is how memory works. But if we keep returning to those places, we keep refreshing the pain. To heal, we must break the loop. We must create **new cues** that trigger **new routines** with **new rewards**.

Why We Must Not Recreate Past Memories

- Going to the same hotel where you once stayed keeps you locked in comparison.
- Eating the same dish from the same stall repeats the old script.
- Walking the same street invites ghosts to join us.

And love is not about ghosts. Love is about presence.
We must stop saying, *"That's where I used to go. That's what I used to eat. That's how it was."*

Instead, we must say, *"This is where we go. This is what we taste. This is who we are."*

Building Brand New Memories

Here is how we build our own treasure chest of memories:

1. **The First Sip Ritual** – I make you chai, not because anyone else did, but because my chai will always remind you of me. The first sip is our private signature.
2. **The New Map Adventure** – Once a month, we pick a spot on the map—big or small—and we go. Not to repeat, but to discover.

3. **The Memory Jar** – Each time we laugh, discover, or share something new, we write it on a slip and place it in a jar. At year's end, we read them aloud.
4. **The "Never Before" List** – We create a list of things neither of us has done—cooking a new dish, exploring a new trail, learning a new game—and we do them together.

By creating fresh memories, we do not just escape the past we **bury it with beauty**.

Scientific Proof: Novelty Heals

Brain research shows that novelty—new experiences—creates dopamine, the chemical of motivation and joy. Couples who explore new activities together report higher satisfaction, deeper intimacy, and stronger bonds.

Psychologist Arthur Aron found that couples who engaged in new and exciting activities together felt more in love than those who only repeated old routines.
This means that our happiness is not in repeating the "best of the past." It is in creating the "never before" of the present.

Our Sacred Rule: Do Not Mix Past and Present

One of the most important vows we make is this:

- We will not compare.
- We will not repeat.
- We will not recycle.

Our love deserves **fresh paint, fresh walls, fresh windows.** No ghost is allowed to sit at our table. No shadow is allowed in our bed. This is not about running from your history. It is about **honouring our present.**

Our Memory-Building Habits

Here are practices that keep our love alive, original, and unforgettable:

- **New Places Rule** – Each time we crave an outing, we choose a new place first. If we must return to an old place, we rewrite it by making it ours new dishes, new laughter, new rituals.

- **Our Signature Dishes** – Foods that belong only to us. Perhaps my special chai, your favourite pasta, or a new dessert we create together. These become our edible love notes.
- **The "First Time Together" Diary** – We document every first: first road trip, first festival, first midnight walk. Each entry is proof that our love is writing new history.

A Letter to You

My beloved, I want you to hear this in your heart: I do not want recycled love. I do not want shadows. I do not want comparisons. I want *you and me.*
Fresh, raw, alive.

Every memory, every habit, every tradition we build—it must belong to us, and us alone. Your past cannot give you what I will. Your past cannot build with you what I will. The past is finished. But with me, the canvas is blank, the paint is wet, the brushes are ready.

We are not just building love. We are building **new worlds of memory.**

Declaration

- No recreating past moments.
- No repeating past tastes.
- No revisiting past ghosts.
- Every memory is new.
- Every habit is ours.
- Every day is a first day.

Our love is not a second-hand garment. It is tailored fresh, sewn with threads of discovery, stitched with laughter, embroidered with new rituals.

Together, we do not recycle.

We **create.**

6

NEVER MIXING PAST & PRESENT

Love is like architecture. Every building has a foundation. If we try to pour new concrete over broken stones without cleaning, the cracks reappear. If we build walls on top of ruins without removing them, the walls shake and fall.

In relationships, the same law applies: **we cannot build the present if we keep mixing it with the past.**

This chapter is the most important blueprint for us. It is the vow that our love will not be built on recycled bricks. It will not be haunted by ghosts. It will not be diluted with comparisons. This is our chapter of **purity and presence.**

---

1. Why We Mix the Past Into the Present

It happens almost unconsciously. A word, a smell, a place, a habit—and suddenly, you are pulled back. The past rushes into the present, like dust blowing into a newly cleaned room.

Psychologists explain this with the concept of **triggers.** Trauma, memories, and emotions are stored not just in the mind but in the body. The brain, in its attempt to protect you, says: *"This feels familiar. It might hurt again. Be careful."*

That's why:

- A certain ringtone can bring anxiety.
- A familiar hotel lobby can bring flashbacks.
- A style of speaking can awaken old pain.

It is not weakness. It is biology. But biology can be re-trained. The mistake would be to let these echoes dominate the present relationship. Because when the past is mixed with the present, three things happen:

1. **Comparison** – "He did this, will you also?"
2. **Suspicion** – "Maybe this will end the same way."
3. **Injustice** – The new love is punished for crimes never committed.

And so, the present is poisoned.

---

2. The Psychology of Pure Presence

The key is learning to live in **psychological presence.**

Eckhart Tolle, in *The Power of Now*, wrote:

"Realize deeply that the present moment is all you ever have. Make the Now the primary focus of your life."

Living in presence means:

- Not dragging old names into new conversations.
- Not rehearsing old betrayals in new arguments.
- Not reliving old journeys while on new ones.

It means allowing the **new person**—me, your husband, your partner—to be experienced as himself, without filters, without shadows.

3. Scientific Proof: The Past is Not the Present

Neuroscience shows that memory is **not a photograph**. Every time you recall it, the brain **reconstructs** it, often adding distortions. This means the past is not a fixed truth—it is a story your brain keeps rewriting.

But the present is alive, breathing, real. The smell of today's chai, the sound of my voice, the way I hold your hand these are not rewrites, these are **real-time experiences.**

If we stay anchored in the present, we create living truth, not recycled illusions.

---

4. The Dangers of Mixing Past & Present

Let us be brutally clear: mixing the past with the present is a form of **self-sabotage.**

- When you say, *"He used to...,"* you reopen wounds.
- When you compare me to him, you dishonour both yourself and me.
- When you repeat his name, you invite him back into your sacred space.

Love cannot grow in divided soil. If half the heart is in yesterday, today withers. This is why we must draw a sacred line: **the past stays buried.**

---

5. The Discipline of Forgetting

Philosopher Friedrich Nietzsche once said:

"Blessed are the forgetful, for they get the better even of their blunders."

Forgetting is not weakness. Forgetting is healing. Forgetting is a conscious act of love.

How do we practice it?

1. **Block & Delete** – Every unnecessary call, every reminder, every lingering contact is cut off. If it brings pain, it has no right to remain.
2. **Name Ban** – No more repeating the name. Words are powerful. Every time you say it, you refresh the wound. Silence it, and it loses power.
3. **Memory Replacement** – Each time an old thought intrudes, immediately replace it with a new shared memory. This is not avoidance—it is rewiring.
4. **Anchoring in the Present** – When triggered, hold something real: my hand, my voice, my kiss. Ground yourself in now.

Forgetting is not erasing—it is choosing not to water weeds.

---

6. New Habits of Thought

To never mix the past with the present, we must train the mind with new affirmations:

- "This man is not my past."
- "This love is not my history."
- "I deserve new joy."
- "I honour today."
- "The future belongs to me and him."

Repeated daily, these phrases carve new grooves in the brain. They weaken the trauma pathways and strengthen the trust ones.

---

7. Love as Sacred Architecture

Think of our love as a home we are designing. Would you bring broken furniture into a newly built house? Would you hang torn curtains on fresh walls? No—you would decorate with new colours, fresh fabric, clean lines.
So too with love. No old names, no old places, no old shadows. Only new. Only fresh. Only ours.

---

8. The Role of Intimacy

One of the most powerful ways to stay in the present is through **intimacy.** In every kiss, every embrace, every shared breath, we remind each other: *This is now. This is us.*
Sexual love becomes an anchor. The sensations are new, the pleasures are new, the experiences are unique to us. No ghost can survive where present passion burns brightly.
When I touch you, when I bring you to heights you never reached before, it is not repetition—it is creation. Each moment is unrepeatable, eternal in its own right.

---

9. Voices From Psychology

- **Carl Jung**: "I am not what happened to me. I am what I choose to become."
- **Erich Fromm**: "Love is an act of faith, and whoever is of little faith is also of little love."

- **Brené Brown**: "Owning our story can be hard but not nearly as difficult as spending our lives running from it."

Their message is unified: the past must be acknowledged, but it must not be carried. Only then can love thrive.

10. Our Covenant of Presence

Beloved, let this be our vow:

- I will never compare you to anyone.
- I will never recall what is buried.
- I will honour only this moment, this life, this us.
- The past is over. The future is ours.

When we design our love, no old bricks are used. Only new materials, stronger, brighter, unbreakable.

11. A Practical Exercise

Tonight, let us do this:

- Write down every place, food, or habit that still ties you to the past.
- Tear the paper into pieces.
- Burn it or throw it away.
- Hold my hand, sip my chai, and say: *"Only us, only now."*

This ritual marks the burial of ghosts and the birth of presence.

The past is a shadow, and shadows vanish when the sun rises.
You are my sunrise.
Our love is the daylight.
No shadow will enter this house.
No ghost will dine at this table.
No echo will disturb our song.
This is the covenant of presence:
You and me, here and now, forever.

7
HEALING FROM TRAUMA OF THE PAST

The human heart is not made of glass—it does not simply shatter once and stay broken. Instead, it remembers. It carries wounds. And when those wounds are not healed, they bleed into the present.

Many women carry scars from relationships where they gave everything—time, love, sacrifice—only to be met with anger, neglect, or selfishness. These scars do not vanish when the relationship ends. They linger.

But trauma is not the final chapter. Healing is possible. In fact, with love, trauma can become the soil from which the strongest growth emerges. This chapter is about understanding those wounds, naming them clearly, and then **rewriting the story together.**

---

1. The Nature of Past Trauma

Psychologists define trauma not only as physical harm but also as **emotional betrayal** repeated over time.

It comes in many forms:

- **Anger:** A partner who uses shouting or rage to control.
- **Neglect:** A partner who withholds time, affection, or presence.
- **Selfishness:** A partner who only takes, never gives.
- **Unhygienic & Immaturity:** A partner who refuses to grow, while the woman tries endlessly to improve him.
- **Exploitation:** A partner who uses her resources—money, care, energy—without giving back.

Each of these leaves behind an invisible wound. And often, women blame themselves: *"Maybe I should have done more. Maybe I expected too much. Maybe it was my fault."*

But the truth is: **trauma is never the victim's fault.**

2. Story: The Silent Neglect

Jyoti sat by the window every evening, waiting. Dinner grew cold, the television hummed in the background. He had promised to come early, but the hours slipped by. When he finally arrived, there was no apology. Only silence. He ate without speaking, scrolled his phone, and then turned his back to her in bed. She cried quietly, but he never noticed. Over time, her tears dried, but her heart hardened. She stopped waiting. She stopped hoping.

This is the trauma of neglect. It whispers: *"You don't matter. Your time doesn't matter. Your heart doesn't matter."*

3. Story: The Anger That Burns

Jyoti asked a simple question: "Can we talk about our plans?" His face darkened. His voice rose. Words like knives filled the room. He slammed doors, threw objects, cursed her for wanting too much. Her body shook—not because she feared losing him, but because she feared losing herself. Still, she stayed, hoping tomorrow would be different. But tomorrow brought more shouting, more rage.

This is the trauma of anger. It tells a woman: *"You must shrink. Your voice is dangerous. Your needs are punishable."*

---

4 Story: The Woman Who Gave Too Much

She worked, she cooked, she cleaned, she comforted. She even gave him money when he failed. She bought his clothes, urged him to study, encouraged him to dream. But he never gave back. He drained her, like a well that never refilled. One day, she looked in the mirror and saw a woman tired, hollow, unloved. She wondered: "Is this love? Or is this slavery?"

This is the trauma of selfishness and exploitation. It convinces her that love means giving without ever receiving.

---

5. Why Trauma Stays

Psychologists explain that trauma lingers because the brain's **amygdala** (the fear centre) stores emotional memory separately from rational thought. Even when you know "It's over," your body still reacts as if it's happening.

That is why:

- A raised voice makes the body tense.
- A late arrival creates panic.
- A request for money awakens old wounds.

The past intrudes into the present—not because you want it, but because your body remembers.

---

6. Healing Through Love

The miracle is that love has the power to heal trauma. Not instantly, not magically, but through **consistent, gentle presence.**

Here is how we replace trauma with trust:

- **Against Neglect → Consistent Attention**

I notice you. I listen. I come when I promise. My presence tells your heart: *You matter.*

- **Against Anger → Calm Tenderness**

Where he shouted, I speak softly. Where he cursed, I bless. My voice tells your body: *You are safe.*

- **Against Selfishness → Generous Giving**

Where he only took, I give freely. Where he drained, I fill. My actions tell your spirit: *You are cherished.*

- **Against Exploitation → Partnership**

Where he used, I build. Where he demanded, I support. My love tells your soul: *We are a team.*

---

7. A Healing Ritual

Tonight, let us create a ritual of healing:

1. Write down one painful sentence from your past (for example: *"I don't matter."*).
2. Then, I will write the opposite truth (for example: *"You are my everything. You are the centre of my world."*).
3. Together, we will burn the paper.
4. And we will speak the truth aloud, so your heart begins to believe it.

---

8. Psychological Voices of Healing

- **Judith Herman**, trauma psychologist: *"Recovery can take place only within the context of relationships. It cannot occur in isolation."*
- **Carl Rogers**: *"The curious paradox is that when I accept myself just as I am, then I can change."*
- **Brené Brown**: *"Shame cannot survive being spoken and met with empathy."*

These voices remind us: you heal not alone, but in the embrace of love.

---

9. Our Personal Healing Journey

My love, I know you gave too much in the past. I know you carried burdens not yours. I know you endured anger, neglect, selfishness, and pain.

But I tell you now: **with me, the story is different.**

I will not neglect you—
I will notice you every day.

I will not shout at you—
I will speak with calm tenderness.

I will not exploit you—
I will build with you.

I will not use you—I will cherish you.
Your trauma ends here. Your healing begins here.

---

10. Story of Renewal: The Tea of Safety

She sat at the table, expecting silence. Instead, he placed a cup of chai in front of her. He didn't just place it; he looked into her eyes and smiled. "This is your cup," he said, "made only for you." She sipped, and tears filled her eyes—not because the tea was perfect, but because, for the first time, she felt seen. The cup was small, but it carried a universe of healing.

This is what new love does. It rewrites old scripts with new rituals.

Declaration

- Trauma ends when love rewrites the story.
- Neglect ends when presence begins.
- Anger ends when tenderness reigns.
- Selfishness ends when generosity flows.
- Exploitation ends when partnership thrives.

My beloved, your scars are not signs of weakness. They are proof of your strength. And with me, they will fade—not erased, but transformed into wisdom.

You are no longer the woman who waits in silence.

You are the woman who is cherished in fullness.

8
EXPLORING THE NEW WORLD TOGETHER

Love is not a cage; it is a passport. When two people commit to building a life together, they are not just agreeing to share a home or a routine. They are agreeing to become explorers—of the world, of each other, and of the infinite possibilities of joy.

Too often, relationships that have been stained by the past become stuck. Old restaurants, old songs, old trips—all haunted by memories. Instead of bringing happiness, they trigger wounds. This is why it is not enough to simply "forget" the past. We must **replace it with something greater.**

Exploration is not only about travel. It is about cultivating curiosity, playfulness, and freshness in love. It is about saying: *"Every day with you is new. Every road we walk is our road."*

---

1. Why Exploration Matters in Healing

2.

Psychologists often speak of the human need for **novelty**. Our brains release dopamine, the "joy chemical," not just from rewards, but from discovering something new.

When couples explore together—whether it's a new café, a new hobby, or a new city—they are not just adding activities. They are **rewiring their emotional bond.** They are teaching the brain to associate love with wonder.

Exploration replaces trauma with excitement. Where old memories once stood like ghosts, new memories bloom like flowers.

---

2. The Principle of "New Maps"

Imagine life as a map. In your past relationship, parts of that map became poisoned. Certain places, foods, or songs are no longer safe. They trigger pain.

The answer is not to force yourself back into those old places. The answer is to **draw new maps.**

- Instead of the old café, find a new one where your laughter fills the air.
- Instead of the old song, discover music together that becomes "ours."
- Instead of repeating past trips, create journeys so breath-taking that the old ones seem small.

The past is not erased, but it is overshadowed—outshined by the brilliance of the present.

3. The Mountain of New Beginnings

There was once a couple who carried heavy shadows. The woman had walked trails before, but they were marked with sorrow. Each hill reminded her of arguments, each river of loneliness.

When she looked at mountains, she did not see beauty, she saw ghosts. One day, her new partner said: *"Let us climb together." She resisted at first. "No,"* she whispered, *"I've been here before. It hurts."* But he took her hand, steady and warm. *"Not here,"* he said. *"Not in the same way. With me, it will be new."*

So they climbed. The path was steep, and sometimes she wanted to stop. Old fears whispered: *"This is just like before. You will suffer again."* But each time, he slowed his steps, matched her pace, and whispered back: *"This is not like before. You are not alone. We are us."*

At the summit, the world opened in every direction valleys, rivers, clouds beneath their feet. She gasped, not only from the view but from the realization: *"This is my first mountain. The first one that is mine. The first one that belongs to us."* Tears filled her eyes, not of grief but of release. In that moment, the old mountains lost their power. They were only shadows now. This summit was brighter than them all.

This story is not just about a mountain. It is about **love's power to turn haunted places into holy places.** Together, you can climb every hill of life and make it new.

---

4. Practical Exploration in Daily Life

Exploration does not always mean airplanes and mountains. It can mean small, everyday acts of discovery:

- **New Food Adventures:** Cook together, try cuisines you've never tasted. Let the kitchen become your playground.
- **New Shops & Cafés:** Walk through markets, sit in hidden cafés, make each outing feel like treasure-hunting.
- **New Music & Books:** Read aloud to each other, discover songs that feel like "our soundtrack."
- **New Routines:** Walk in a park at sunrise. Try yoga together. Build a ritual of tea in the evening.
- **New Creativity:** Paint, dance, write. Create something that is not perfect but personal.

Every new act is a seed planted in the soil of your relationship.

---

4. Psychological Insight: The "Novelty Effect"

Dr. Arthur Aron, a psychologist who studied love and intimacy, found that couples who engage in novel activities together report **higher levels of satisfaction and closeness**. This is because novelty stimulates the brain's reward system, making partners associate love with excitement and joy. In other words: **when we explore together, we fall in love again.**

6. Your Personal Declaration

My love, I do not wish to repeat the past. I do not want our life to be a copy of old scripts. I want to build a world with you that is so rich, so full of wonder, that you never look back. With me:

- Old hotels will be replaced by new journeys.
- Old cafés will be replaced by fresh laughter.
- Old memories will be replaced by dazzling adventures.

The world is vast, and we will taste it together. Each corner of the map will carry one name only—*ours.*

---

7. Closing Vision

Picture us years from now. We sit together with photo albums and memories. But there are no shadows. Each page glows with our smiles, our journeys, our explorations. We are not bound to old roads. We are travelers, lovers, explorers. And the greatest discovery we ever made was not a mountain, a sea, or a city—it was **each other.**

9
BLOCKING TRAUMA, UNBLOCKING LOVE

Trauma is like a shadow—it follows until you shine a stronger light. That light is not just forgetting, but **blocking, setting boundaries, and choosing love actively.**
This chapter is about how to keep the past truly in the past, how to seal the door to hurt, and how to open the door to joy.

1. The Art of Blocking Trauma

Psychology teaches us about **cognitive closure**—the need to resolve unfinished emotional business. If past relationships remain half-open doors (calls, messages, memories revisited), healing stalls.
Blocking is not cruelty; it is medicine.

- **Block calls and contacts** that bring distress.
- **Block mental repetitions**—do not say their name, do not replay their habits.
- **Block association triggers** by making new rituals, new songs, new meals.

This is called **boundary-setting**. In Attachment Theory (John Bowlby), healthy love requires **safe boundaries**—knowing what is *inside* (us, our bond) and what is *outside* (the past, old ghosts).

2.: The Festival of Renewal

After the mountain climb, the couple returned home. The woman felt lighter, but shadows still tried to follow her. Some nights, she dreamed of old voices. Some days, a ringtone made her heart race. She confessed: *"What if the past comes back?"*
He smiled gently and said: *"Then we will sing louder than the past."*

That evening, he lit candles, placed two cups of tea on the table, and played soft music. He reached for her hand and whispered: *"Let's dance."* She laughed shyly. *"Here? In the kitchen?" "Yes,"* he said, *"especially here."* They swayed clumsily at first, but soon the rhythm carried them. She rested her head on his chest, and for the first time in years, her body felt safe in movement. The past could not enter their dance.

Afterward, he cooked for her simple, but with care. He placed each dish before her like a treasure, smiling as if to say: *"Your nourishment is my joy."* She tasted, and it was more than food; it was love disguised as flavor.

Later that night, he warmed oil in his palms and gently massaged her shoulders. Each stroke whispered: *"You are safe. You are loved. You are mine."* Her body, once stiff with old fear, melted under his touch. He asked for nothing in return. His love was pure giving, without demand. She wept, not from sadness, but from the overwhelming truth: this was love she had never known before. Love that did not take. Love that gave.

2. What Is Love?

Psychologists and poets alike have tried to define love. Here, we bring together science and soul:

- **Erich Fromm**, in *The Art of Loving*: *"Love is an activity, not a passive affect; it is a standing in, not a falling for."* Love is *doing*, not just *feeling.*

- **C.S. Lewis**: Love is *agape*—selfless, unconditional care.

- **Biological science**: Love floods the brain with **oxytocin** (the bonding hormone), released during touch, massage, eye contact, and even singing together. This is why small rituals of affection matter.

- **Attachment Theory**: Love creates a **secure base**—a partner who says, *"Go explore the world, I'll be here when you return."*

So, what is love?

- Love is cooking chai just to see your smile.
- Love is dancing in the kitchen without music.
- Love is massaging your tired body without expecting anything back.
- Love is singing together off-key, laughing more than listening.
- Love is carrying your pain until it feels lighter.
- Love is not keeping score.

4. The Psychology of Playfulness in Love

Relationship researcher **John Gottman** found that couples who remain playful—singing, dancing, teasing, exploring—stay happier and more resilient. Play is not childish. Play is **bonding.** When he sang to her, when she laughed at his clumsy dance, when they cooked together—it wasn't about the action, it was about saying: *"With you, I am safe enough to be silly."* That is the highest form of intimacy.

---

5. Pampering and Care as Healing

True love is not grand declarations only. It is small acts repeated daily:

- Making her tea the way she likes.
- Oil massage after a long day.
- Cooking her favorite meal.
- Running fingers through her hair until she falls asleep.
- Covering her with a blanket when she dozes off.

Each act may seem small, but together they say: *"Your comfort is my priority."* This is called **compassionate love**—love that seeks the well-being of the other without demand. In psychology, compassionate love is the strongest predictor of lasting, fulfilling relationships.

6. The Declaration of Selfless Love

My love, I do not give to you because I expect return. I do not sing to hear applause. I do not massage to earn favor. I do not cook to be thanked.

I give because giving to you is my joy.
Your smile is my reward.
Your peace is my victory.
Your healing is my success.
I love you not for what you give me, but for what I can give you.

7. Closing Vision: Unlocking Love

Blocking trauma is only the first step. Once the past is silenced, love becomes music. And when love is music, two people become instruments different tones, but one song. You and I are that song. We will sing, we will dance, we will laugh, we will cook, we will care. We will live love as an **art of giving.** And in this, the past cannot follow. The shadows cannot dance. Only light remains.

10
LOVE IN THE RHYTHM OF WORK

Jyoti used to hate the word *"office."* For her, it meant loneliness. In the past, office hours were hours of neglect long stretches where her partner forgot she even existed. He never called. He never checked in. Work was his excuse to vanish.

But with him this new man, her true partner the office became something else entirely. It became another place where love lived.

Morning Ritual

He rose early, not rushing, but with quiet joy. Before opening his laptop, he brewed her chai. The steam curled in the air, carrying cardamom and comfort. He placed it by her hand with a smile that said: *"Even in work, you are my priority."* She laughed and teased*: "You treat me like a queen."* He replied softly*: "Because you are."*

Before leaving for office, he kissed her forehead not a distracted gesture, but a promise: *"I will return. I am always with you."* That kiss lingered longer than any perfume.

Midday Connection

At the office, in the middle of meetings and deadlines, he did not forget. He sent her a simple message: *"Lunch? Don't forget to eat."*

Sometimes it was just an emoji of a heart, sometimes a photo of his coffee with a note: *"Wish you were here."* Each ping on her phone was like a heartbeat reminding her: I matter. I am seen.

On busier days, he made time for a short video call. She would see him in his chair, tie slightly loosened, exhaustion in his eyes—but his smile was only for her. *"How are you?"* he asked, voice soft despite the chaos around him. She would reply*: "I miss you."* He would laugh and say: *"I miss you too, but look—just a few hours, and I'm back in your arms."* That reassurance made even the longest hours bearable.

Evening Return

When the workday ended, he did not collapse into silence or distraction. He came home with stories. He shared the little victories, the funny office moments, even the stress—but always in a way that included her. She was not an outsider to his work; she was his confidante. Together, over tea or dinner, they laughed about colleagues, dreamed about future plans, or simply rested in the comfort of togetherness.

Sometimes, he would surprise her by cooking after work. Even if it was simple—an omelette, noodles, or cutting fruit—it was not about the food. It was about saying*: "Even when I am tired, I still choose to care for you."*

Nighttime Pampering

On nights when she felt the weight of her own work, he brought out warm oil. *"Sit,"* he whispered. He massaged her shoulders, her neck, her tired hands.

The office stress melted under his touch. *"You deserve rest,"* he murmured, *"and I'll make sure you get it."* Sometimes they ended the day not with talk, but with gentle music, swaying together in a slow, quiet dance under the dim light of their room.

And as she drifted to sleep, her last thought was not of past men, not of old ghosts. It was only of him the man who redesigned not just her love, but her daily life.

The Technical Truth of Love in Daily Life

This kind of love may sound poetic, but it is grounded in **real psychological science**:

- **Attachment Theory (Bowlby):** Regular check-ins (texts, calls, video chats) create a *secure base*. She knows: even when you are away, you are with her.
- **Behavioral Psychology:** Small, consistent reinforcements (chai, messages, massages) build a loop of safety and joy.
- **Neurobiology:** Video calls, even digital, trigger oxytocin release when faces and voices are exchanged. Touch (massages, hugs) further deepens the bond.
- **Relationship Science (Gottman):** Couples who share "daily stories" (even about work) build emotional intimacy. Love is not in grand moments—it's in the *ordinary, done with care.*

Redesigning the Dream World

Love that lives in daily rituals becomes so powerful that it rewires even the subconscious. Slowly, the brain stops associating *office = neglect* and starts associating *office = care*.

That is why now, even in dreams, she no longer remembers the men of the past. Her mind does not wander to them, because her present is so rich, so complete, that it fills her entirely.

Her dreams, once haunted, are now gardens of safety. And in those dreams, he is always there—sometimes cooking, sometimes dancing, sometimes just holding her hand.

This is what **Redesign 2.0** truly means: not only in waking life, but even in the dreamworld, love belongs only to us.

Final Declaration

My love, I do not want to be your distraction from the past. I want to be your **entire future.**

I want your days filled with my voice, your nights filled with my touch, your dreams filled with my presence.

I want your office hours to echo with my messages, your evenings to glow with my laughter, your mornings to begin with my chai. With me, you will never again measure love in absence.

ABOUT THE AUTHOR

The author serves as a government officer, where discipline, dedication, and responsibility shape his daily life. Beyond his official duties, he carries a deep passion for understanding the human heart and the psychology of relationships. Redesigning Us is his heartfelt contribution—an exploration of how love, when guided by trust and compassion, can overcome past struggles and flourish into something new and powerful.